A Note from Michelle about
THE BABY-SITTING BOSS

Hi! I'm Michelle Tanner. I'm nine years old. And I totally want to be a baby-sitter. There's just one problem. My whole family thinks I'm too young. Can you believe it? That's why I have to come up with a plan. A plan that is so awesome it will change everybody's mind. But it's not going to be easy. Because my family is huge!

There's my dad and my two older sisters, D.J. and Stephanie. But that's not all.

My mom died when I was little. So my uncle Jesse moved in to help Dad take care of us. So did Joey Gladstone. He's my dad's friend from college. It's almost like having three dads. But that's still not all!

First Uncle Jesse got married to Becky Donaldson. Then they had twin boys, Nicky and Alex. The twins are four years old now. And they're so cute.

That's nine people. And our dog, Comet, makes ten. Sure, it gets kind of crazy sometimes. But I wouldn't change it for anything. It's so much fun living in a full house!

FULL HOUSE™ MICHELLE novels

Available from MINSTREL Books

FULL HOUSE™
Michelle

The Baby-sitting Boss

Cathy East Dubowski

A Parachute Book

A MINSTREL® BOOK

Published by POCKET BOOKS
New York   London   Toronto   Sydney   Tokyo   Singapore

A MINSTREL PAPERBACK *Original*

A Minstrel Book published by
POCKET BOOKS, a division of Simon & Schuster Inc.
1230 Avenue of the Americas, New York, NY 10020

A PARACHUTE BOOK

Copyright © and ™ 1999 by Warner Bros.

ISBN: 0-671-02156-7

First Minstrel Books printing May 1999

10 9 8 7 6 5 4 3 2 1

A MINSTREL BOOK and colophon are registered trademarks of Simon & Schuster Inc.

Cover photo by Schultz Photography

Printed in the U.S.A.

The Baby-sitting Boss

Chapter 1

♥ "Look at that!" nine-year-old Michelle Tanner cried as she dashed toward a clothing store across the mall.

Three matching blue T-shirts dangled from hangers in the display window. Each one had a drawing of three girls holding hands on the front.

"Cool!" said Cassie Wilkins, Michelle's best friend.

"Awesome!" said Mandy Metz, her other best friend.

Michelle blew her strawberry-blond bangs

out of her eyes. "Come on," she told her friends. "Let's try them on!"

Michelle, Mandy, and Cassie ran inside the store. A teenage salesgirl was behind a cash register. She had long blond hair and wore a white shirt and jeans.

"Can we try on the T-shirts in the window?" Michelle asked excitedly.

The salesgirl popped her gum. "Sure." She removed the shirts from the window and handed them to Michelle.

Michelle and her friends raced to the dressing room.

"I love it!" Mandy squealed as she pulled a T-shirt over her head.

"Me, too!" Cassie cried.

Michelle gazed into a big mirror. Then Mandy and Cassie stood next to her. The three friends smiled and held hands, just like the girls on the T-shirts.

"These are perfect!" Michelle declared. "We could all wear them on the same day. Then *everybody* would know we're best friends." She glanced at the price tag. "Uh-oh."

"What?" Mandy and Cassie asked at the same time.

"These shirts cost twenty dollars each!" Michelle exclaimed. "How much money do you guys have?" Michelle knew that *she* didn't have enough money to buy a T-shirt.

Mandy pulled out three dollar bills from her backpack. "Not enough," she said with a sigh.

Cassie dug out her wallet and showed her friends. "Me either."

"Maybe we could save up for them," Mandy suggested.

Michelle shook her head. "If we don't get these now, somebody's sure to buy one. Then we won't match."

Cassie ran her hand over the shirt. "But what can we do?"

Michelle gazed at the T-shirt in the mirror once more. Suddenly she had an idea. "Sometimes Stephanie and D.J. buy things on layaway," she announced.

"What's that?" Mandy asked.

"If you don't have enough money to buy something, you can pay for only part of it," Michelle explained. "Then the store holds it for you until you pay off the rest. That way nobody else can buy it."

"That's a great idea!" Cassie said. "Let's do it!"

The girls quickly changed back into their regular clothes. Then they raced to the cash register and laid the T-shirts on the counter. When they put all their money together, they had just enough to put them on layaway.

The salesgirl popped her gum again. "I can hold them for two weeks."

"Two weeks?" Michelle exclaimed. "That's not a long time!"

The salesgirl shrugged. "That's the rule. If you don't come back and pay by then, we have to put the shirts back on the rack."

"How are we each going to get twenty dollars in two weeks?" Cassie moaned. "It's impossible!"

Mandy sighed. "I wish I could get a job or something."

"Hey. That's a great idea, Mandy!" Michelle cried.

"Yeah," Cassie agreed. "I bet my dad would pay me to wash his car."

"My mom *might* give me money to do laundry," Mandy said.

Michelle wrinkled her nose. "That's a lot

of work. I want to do something that's easy."

But what? she wondered.

"I know," Michelle announced. "I'm going to baby-sit. I've been helping Aunt Becky look after Nicky and Alex ever since they were born. It's *super* easy!"

Michelle turned to the salesgirl. "We'll be back in two weeks," she told her.

Then Michelle grabbed Cassie's and Mandy's hands. "Come on," she said, pulling them out of the store. "We've got to make some money—fast!"

Chapter 2

♥   These signs are *awesome!* Michelle told herself later that day. She popped the cap back on her marker and looked over her work.

BABY-SITTER FOR HIRE

4 YEARS EXPERIENCE

SPECIALTY—TWINS!

Michelle smiled to herself. Now all I have to do is put these up, she thought. Then people will want me to watch their kids, and I'll earn the money for my T-shirt.

"Michelle, time for dinner!" her father called from downstairs.

"Coming!" Michelle gathered her signs and carried them to the kitchen. She wanted to show them to her family.

Her father, Danny, was serving one of his latest creations—*meatless* meat loaf. Her two older sisters, Stephanie and D.J., were setting glasses on the table.

Joey Gladstone, her dad's best friend, was arranging a platter of fruit slices into a funny face. Joey always did things like that. He was a comedian. He lived in the basement apartment. He moved into the Tanner home to help out after Michelle's mom died. That was a long time ago.

"I'm going to get you guys!" Michelle heard Uncle Jesse say with a laugh.

Uncle Jesse and Aunt Becky chased their four-year-old twins, Nicky and Alex, into the kitchen.

Uncle Jesse moved in to help out the family, too. Then he married Aunt Becky. And *then* they had Nicky and Alex. They all live on the third floor of the Tanner home.

"Look, everybody," Michelle announced after all nine of them were sitting at the table. She held up one of her signs.

"Four years experience?" Joey hooted. "Michelle, four years ago you were only five!"

"Yeah, four years ago we used to baby-sit *you,*" Uncle Jesse added with a chuckle.

Stephanie snickered as she passed some mashed potatoes.

Michelle frowned. She didn't like the way everyone was laughing. They were supposed to be impressed!

"So?" she replied. "I've been helping Aunt Becky with the twins since they were born. Right, Aunt Becky?"

Aunt Becky gave Michelle a quick hug. "Sure you have. And I couldn't have done it without you."

"See?" Michelle said.

"Michelle, honey, that's not quite the same thing as baby-sitting all by yourself," her father pointed out. "Stephanie and D.J. didn't baby-sit until they were much older than you."

"But they didn't have Nicky and Alex," Michelle argued.

"Give it up, Michelle," D.J. said. "You're way too little to baby-sit."

"Besides," Stephanie added, "nobody will hire you. You don't have any references."

"References?" Michelle asked.

"You know," Stephanie explained. "A list of people who say you're a good sitter."

"How do I get references?" Michelle asked.

"By baby-sitting," D.J. replied.

Michelle sighed. "But Stephanie just said I can't baby-sit unless I have references. And you say I can't get references unless I baby-sit! It doesn't make sense!"

Stephanie shrugged. "It's kind of hard to explain, Michelle. You'll understand when you're older."

Michelle groaned. At this rate she was never going to get a baby-sitting job. It wasn't fair!

"I'm sorry, Michelle," her father said. "You're just not old enough to baby-sit yet. And that's my final word."

Michelle opened her mouth to argue some more, but Danny gave her a look. A look that said *case closed!*

After dinner Michelle helped clear the

table. How can I get the money for my T-shirt if I can't baby-sit? she wondered.

Then she had a horrible thought. What if Cassie and Mandy earned enough money to buy *their* shirts—and she didn't? She would feel so left out when they wore them!

She had to think up another way to earn the money. She just *had* to!

Chapter

3

♡ Michelle ran upstairs to her room. She grabbed a small notepad and pen from her desk and flopped down on her bed. *I need a new idea—fast!*

She wrote at the top of the page:

NEW IDEAS FOR EARNING MONEY

But all Michelle could think of was *Baby-sitting, baby-sitting, baby-sitting!*

"I know I'd be a good baby-sitter," she

grumbled. "But how can I if Dad won't let me?"

"Jesse!" Michelle heard Aunt Becky holler from the bathroom on the third floor. "Can you help? I'm up to my elbows in bubble bath. And I need more towels for the twins!"

"I'll get them!" Michelle jumped off her bed and stuffed her notepad and pencil into the back pocket of her jeans. She liked to help Aunt Becky with the twins. Even if she wasn't *really* baby-sitting them.

Michelle raced to the hall closet for towels. Seconds later she skidded to a stop in the upstairs bathroom. "Room service," she announced.

Aunt Becky laughed. "Michelle, you're a lifesaver." She took the extra towels. Then she reached for the shampoo.

Alex squirmed and splashed in the tub.

"Now, Alex, sit still," Aunt Becky said.

"I'll help," Michelle said. She showed the twins how to make bubble bath beards while Aunt Becky shampooed their hair.

Then Michelle helped her aunt dry off the twins and put on their pajamas. "I'm pretty good at baths, don't you think?"

Aunt Becky grinned as she pulled a pajama top over Nicky's head. "You're wonderful, Michelle."

"Really?" Michelle's eyes lit up. She had an idea. An idea about how to get references. Once she has enough of them, she'll show them to Dad. Then he'll *have* to let her baby-sit!

Michelle pulled out her notepad and scribbled down what Aunt Becky said. Then she helped Aunt Becky carry the squirming kids to their room.

"We want a bedtime story!" Nicky shouted.

Aunt Becky delivered Nicky into Uncle

Jesse's arms. "Daddy will read you one," she replied.

"But, Becky," Jesse protested, waving a piece of paper. "I'm in the middle of writing a song. It could be my big hit!"

"I've got my book club meeting tonight, remember?" Aunt Becky asked.

"Oh, that's right." Uncle Jesse sighed.

The twins hugged their mother. Then Becky left the room.

Uncle Jesse stuffed his song into his back pocket.

"Uncle Jesse," Michelle said, still holding Alex. "I'll read the twins their bedtime story."

"Really? Uncle Jesse asked. "You don't mind?"

"No way," Michelle declared. "I love reading bedtime stories."

"Yay!" Nicky yelled.

"We want Michelle," Alex cried.

Uncle Jesse ran a hand through his thick black hair. "Thanks, Michelle." He gave each boy a hug and a tickle. "Be good for your cousin." He went downstairs, humming, and scribbling on his scrap of paper.

Michelle picked out one of her favorite storybooks. Then she and both twins snuggled into Nicky's bed.

I'll show them, Michelle thought. I'll show everybody I'm the greatest baby-sitter a little kid could have!

"'Once upon a time, in the land of dragons . . .'" she read aloud. Michelle tried to make the story exciting. She made up silly voices for the dragon and the witch.

Nicky and Alex laughed.

"Read it again, Michelle," Nicky said when she had finished.

"Read it a *zillion* times!" Alex cried.

"So, you guys think I'm pretty good at reading bedtime stories?" Michelle asked.

"Yes!" Nicky exclaimed, clapping his hands.

"The *best!*" Alex agreed.

Michelle pulled out her pad and made another note. Then she turned back to the first page of the storybook. This time she lowered her voice so that it was soft and sleepy-sounding.

The twins' eyes started to droop. By the time Michelle reached the last page, both boys were fast asleep.

Michelle carefully slid out of the bed just as Uncle Jesse came into the room.

"Michelle, how are the—" He stopped when he saw the boys sleeping. "Way to go, Michelle!" he whispered. He picked up Alex and tucked him into his own bed.

Michelle and Jesse tiptoed out into the hall.

"Uncle Jesse," Michelle whispered. "I'm pretty good at putting little kids to bed, don't you think?"

"Awesome!" Uncle Jesse whispered back.

Michelle pulled out her notebook and wrote down what he said, too.

With a big grin, she bounded down the stairs. She found her father at the kitchen table, looking through a new cookbook.

"Dad, I have references!" Michelle said excitedly. She sat across from Danny. "Now I can be a baby-sitter!"

Danny took off his reading glasses. "References?"

"Yes! Listen." Michelle opened her notepad and read. "One. Becky Donaldson-Katsopolis: 'Michelle is wonderful at giving little kids their baths.'" She grinned at her dad, then went on. "Two. Alex and Nicky Katsopolis: 'Michelle is the best at reading bedtime stories.' And three. Jesse Katsopolis: 'Michelle is awesome at putting little kids to bed.'"

"Doesn't that show I'd make a good baby-sitter, Dad?" Michelle asked.

"I think you'd make an excellent baby-sitter—"

"Yippee!" Michelle could hardly believe her ears.

"Someday!" her father continued.

"But—" Michelle started to say.

Danny shook his head. "I'm sorry, Michelle. But you're just too young to baby-sit."

Michelle slowly climbed the stairs to her room. She lay down on her bed and stared at the ceiling. "It's not fair," she mumbled.

Cassie and Mandy will get their cool T-shirts. They'll both wear them to school on the same day. And everyone will know that *they're* best friends. I'll be the only one left out!

Stephanie came into the room they shared and began to change for bed.

Michelle sat up. "Stephanie, are you baby-sitting this week?"

"Yup," Stephanie pulled her nightgown on over her head. "Tomorrow afternoon at the Andersons'. And on Saturday for the Johnsons."

"Wow," Michelle said, flopping back on her pillow. Two baby-sitting jobs in one week. Stephanie must be making tons of money.

Stephanie tossed Michelle a book.

"What's this?" Michelle asked, sitting up again.

"It's a baby-sitting handbook. Read up. You might learn something by the time you're old enough to baby-sit."

A book? Michelle thought. She flipped through the pages and tossed it aside. Then she picked up her list of references.

Everyone says I'm great with Nicky and Alex, Michelle thought. I know everything there is to know about taking care of little kids.

Now, if only I could figure out a way to prove it!

Chapter

4

♥ "I already earned five dollars washing my mom's and dad's cars," Cassie reported cheerfully the next day at school. She took a bite of her cafeteria lunch. "And I found another eighty-three cents when I cleaned out the inside. And my parents let me keep it!"

"My mom hates doing the laundry," Mandy told her friends. "She said she'd pay me two dollars for every load I wash, dry, and fold."

"Wow," Michelle murmured. "That's a lot

of laundry." Mandy's family was almost as big as Michelle's.

Mandy grinned and unwrapped a granola bar from her lunch bag. "I figure I'll have enough money to finish paying for my T-shirt by the end of the week!"

Michelle took a bite of her meatless meat loaf sandwich and sighed. "You guys are so lucky! If I could just get *one* big baby-sitting job, I'd have enough to get my shirt."

"Michelle!" Cassie exclaimed. "Forget about baby-sitting. Think of something else."

"I can't," Michelle said. "I know I'd be good at it. I just don't get it. What's the big deal about baby-sitting? How hard could it be?"

Mandy tucked a strand of long, curly dark hair behind her ear. "Maybe it's harder than you think," she suggested.

"Maybe . . ." Then Michelle remembered something. "Stephanie's baby-sitting this afternoon!" she announced.

Cassie shrugged. "So?"

"So meet me at my house after school. I've got a plan." Michelle leaned forward. "And *you* guys are going to help me!"

"Are you sure about this?" Mandy asked as she and Cassie walked into Michelle's bedroom later that day.

"Sure I'm sure," Michelle replied. "Stephanie is baby-sitting two houses away. We'll go over there and watch. Then we'll find out once and for all what's so hard about baby-sitting."

"What's in there?" Cassie asked, pointing to the big paper bag resting on Michelle's bed.

Michelle opened the bag and pulled out three pairs of dark sunglasses. "Here, put these on. I found them in the closet down-stairs." Next she pulled out three baseball caps—one for each girl to wear.

"Why?" Cassie wanted to know.

"We need them," Michelle said with a smile. "We're spying, right?" She slipped on her sunglasses and stuffed her hair up under her baseball cap.

Cassie and Mandy giggled as they put on their glasses and hats, too. Then the three girls sneaked to the house where Stephanie was baby-sitting.

Michelle heard laughter. She pushed her back against the side of the house and glanced toward the backyard. She waved to her friends. "Follow me."

Michelle, Cassie, and Mandy crept behind a long row of flowery bushes that lined the side of the house. Soon they were near the backyard.

"My nose is itchy," Mandy said, rubbing it with her hand. "These flowers make me want to sneeze."

"Shhh! Stephanie will hear us." Michelle shoved her sunglasses up on her nose. Then she peeked through the bushes into the back-yard.

Michelle watched as Stephanie and little Marissa Anderson played on the swings. Stephanie gave Marissa a big push.

"Whee!" the little girl squealed, and the two of them laughed.

"Some tough job!" Michelle whispered to her friends. "Stephanie is just pushing a swing. That's not hard."

Then Stephanie grabbed Marissa's hand. The two of them went inside the house.

"Now what?" Cassie asked Michelle.

"This way," Michelle said. With Mandy and Cassie close behind, she hurried up the side of the house and gazed into a window.

Stephanie and Marissa were sitting on the floor playing video games in the family room.

"Big deal!" Michelle whispered. "I'm good at video games."

Later Stephanie and the little girl left the room.

Michelle and her friends ran to another window, and Michelle looked inside. Stephanie and Marissa were in the kitchen.

"What are they doing now?" Cassie asked.

"Eating ice cream," Michelle whispered. "I can do that. I love ice cream!" She stepped away from the window. "This is a total joke! All Stephanie does is play and eat snacks." She planted her hands on her hips. "I *know* I can do *that!*"

"I don't see Stephanie anymore," Mandy

said, gazing through the window. "Where do you think she went?"

Michelle peeked through the window again. Stephanie was nowhere to be found. "I don't know," she whispered.

"I do," Cassie cried. "She's coming this way. Hide!"

Michelle, Cassie, and Mandy quickly ducked back into the bushes.

Michelle held her breath as her sister came closer. Would Stephanie find them?

She watched Stephanie walk up and down the side of the house. Finally, Stephanie shrugged and turned to go inside.

Michelle sighed. That was close, she thought.

"Michelle," Mandy whispered. "These smelly flowers are tickling my nose again."

Michelle stared at Mandy in horror.

"Don't sneeze," she whispered. "Whatever you do, don't—"

"AAAAHHHHH-CHOOOOOOOO!"

Stephanie whirled around and ran back to the bushes. "Come out here, Michelle!" she shouted. "I know you're in there!"

Chapter
5

♥ Michelle and her friends slowly crept out of the bushes.

"I thought I heard your voice!" Stephanie exclaimed. "What were you doing in there, Michelle?"

Michelle didn't know what to say. She was a little embarrassed. But she was angry, too.

"I found out your secret!" she blurted out. "Baby-sitting isn't hard. It's easy—and fun! You just don't want me to do it because I might steal all the baby-sitting jobs away from you!"

Stephanie rolled her eyes. "You think it's so easy, huh?" Stephanie asked.

Michelle crossed her arms and nodded.

"Fine," Stephanie said. "The next time I baby-sit, you can be my assistant. Then you'll see how easy it *isn't!*"

"All right!" Michelle cheered.

"In fact . . ." Stephanie grinned. "I'm baby-sitting Janie Johnson on Saturday. I'll make a deal with you."

"A deal?" Michelle asked, squinting at her sister. "What kind of deal?"

"You help me baby-sit," Stephanie explained. "If you do a good job, I'll tell Dad. And I'll split the money with you, too. If I *don't* think you did a good job, then you have to . . . make my bed for two whole weeks!"

Michelle thought for a moment. She knew Janie. The little girl was two years old, and really sweet! She would be *easy* to take care of.

This is my big chance, Michelle decided. Stephanie will see just how great I am at baby-sitting. Then she can help me talk Dad into letting me baby-sit all by myself!

"Well?" Stephanie asked.

"Okay." Michelle shook Stephanie's hand. "It's a deal!"

"Ouch!" Michelle cried as Stephanie poked her in the ribs. "What was that for?"

It was Saturday morning. Michelle and Stephanie were standing on the Johnsons' porch, ready to start their baby-sitting job.

"I was just reminding you to stand up straight," Stephanie said. She rang the bell.

"How's this?" Michelle asked. She stood up as straight as she could and smiled.

Stephanie giggled. "On second thought, just be yourself."

Michelle relaxed.

"Did you read the baby-sitting book I gave you?" Stephanie asked.

Michelle glanced at her sneakers. She hadn't read a word. Aunt Becky, Uncle Jesse, and the twins had given her all those references. She didn't need to read it. "Well . . . I, uh—"

The door swung open. "Hello, girls!" Mrs. Johnson exclaimed. A little girl with blond curls peeked out shyly from behind her mother. She was wearing a pink outfit with tiny colored teddy bears printed all over it.

She's so cute, Michelle thought. She leaned over and smiled. "Hi, Janie."

Janie grinned and slipped her thumb in her mouth.

Michelle stood up straight. "How are you, Mrs. Johnson?" she asked politely. She hoped that sounded grown-up.

"I'm fine, thanks," Mrs. Johnson said. "It's nice to see you again, Michelle. Janie is excited she's getting *two* baby-sitters today! I know you'll all have so much fun." She turned to her daughter. "Janie, can you say 'Michelle'?" she asked.

Janie grinned shyly. Then she pulled her thumb out of her mouth. "Shell," she said softly.

"Come on, Donna," Mr. Johnson called from the door that led to the garage. "We're going to be late if we don't hurry."

"Coming, Frank." She turned back to Stephanie and Michelle. "Now, Stephanie, as usual, all the emergency numbers are by the phone—including the number where we'll be. Please call us if you have any problems. I might call to check on you guys, too. Okay?"

"No problem, Mrs. Johnson," Stephanie said with a big smile. "Have a good time."

Mrs. Johnson knelt down and gave Janie a big kiss and hug. "Bye, sweetheart. Mommy will be home soon. Be a good girl for Stephanie and Michelle. Okay?"

Janie hugged her mom, then stuck her thumb in her mouth.

As soon as Mr. and Mrs. Johnson were gone, Stephanie picked up Janie and led Michelle into the living room. "Okay, assistant. Time to start baby-sitting," she said. "Get to work. I'm going to watch TV."

Michelle wanted to say *That's not fair!* But she didn't. She had to prove that she was a good baby-sitter.

"What do I do first?" she asked Stephanie. "Play a game? Read Janie a story?"

"Better start at the bottom." Stephanie wrinkled her nose and handed the baby to Michelle. "As in—*change her diaper! Quick!*"

Chapter 6

♥   Michelle gasped. Change Janie's diaper? *Gross!*

She held Janie out at arm's length and stared into her big blue eyes.

Janie smiled back.

Michelle remembered when Nicky and Alex wore diapers. But she was a lot younger then. Aunt Becky or Uncle Jesse usually did *that* part.

"Do I have to?" Michelle asked.

"You want to be a baby-sitter or not?"

Stephanie demanded. She shrugged. "Hey, I'd be glad to keep all the money—"

"No! Wait!" Michelle cried. "I'll do it!"

How hard could it be? she thought. You take one off. You put another one on. . . .

"So." Michelle looked around. "Where's the—you know—stuff?"

Stephanie shrugged. "You're the baby-sitter, Michelle. Figure it out."

Michelle looked around. Hmmm, where would diapers be? In the bathroom?

She carried Janie down the hall and opened a door. Oops! Linen closet. Any diapers in here? Nope.

Michelle tried the next door down. This is it! The hall bathroom. But there was no sign of any diapers.

She heard Stephanie snicker. "Need help, Michelle?"

"No!" Michelle said, embarrassed.

"Janie's just . . . showing me around the house."

Stephanie laughed out loud.

That made Michelle even more determined to figure things out all by herself.

Maybe . . . in Janie's bedroom? Michelle hurried into the baby's room. In one corner a Mother Goose mobile hung over a pretty white crib with ruffly pink covers.

Along the opposite wall stood a little pink bookcase and a white dresser with a changing table on top. A pink ruffly diaper bag hung from the side.

"Okay, sweetie," Michelle said to Janie. She tried to lift Janie up onto the padded changing table. But Janie was too heavy.

"This changing table is too high," she told her. Michelle carried the baby over to the middle of the room. She grabbed a soft green quilt and laid it out on the floor.

Michelle helped the little girl lie down. Then she gently pulled off the toddler's pink teddy bear pants to get to the diaper.

There were little tape tabs holding the diaper together. She pulled at them. They came off pretty easily.

Janie started kicking her legs.

Now what? Michelle wondered. Janie was lying on an unhooked soggy diaper. How do you get the baby off the diaper?

She tried tugging the diaper out from under Janie. But Michelle couldn't get it loose.

Janie laughed and kicked harder.

"Uh, now, now, Janie," Michelle said. She took Janie by the ankles and lifted her an inch. Then she scooted the diaper out from under her.

"Yuck-y!" Michelle balled up the soggy diaper and used the tapes to hold it together.

"What do I do with it?" She spotted a trash can next to the changing table. Maybe I can toss it in from here, she thought.

She aimed, she threw. . . . *Splat!*

The diaper hit the wall and thudded to the floor next to the can. Michelle winced. She'd take care of that in a minute.

Michelle turned back to Janie. Now what? Clean the baby. But the wipes and fresh diapers were on the other side of the room.

With a sigh, Michelle got up to get them. Then Janie jumped up and ran, giggling, out of the room.

"Janie! Come back here!" Michelle chased Janie into the living room.

Stephanie shrieked with laughter. "Naked baby on the loose! Quick! Dial 911!" Michelle ran after Janie. At last she caught her and carried her back to her room.

Always have all the diaper stuff ready

before you start to change the diaper,
Michelle reminded herself.

First Michelle cleaned Janie. Then still
holding her, Michelle grabbed a diaper from
the diaper bag. She unfolded it, then gently
lifted Janie by the ankles again.

See? she thought. I'm definitely getting
the hang of it.

She scooted the diaper under Janie. Then
she folded it up over her tummy. "So far, so
good." Next she undid one of the sticky tapes
and folded it over. Then she did the other tape.

"Shell!" Janie cheered.

"Thanks, kiddo!" Then, just as she was
about to get Janie all wrapped up again—

Oh, no! *"Janie!"* Michelle cried.

Her diaper was all wet again!

Janie giggled. Michelle groaned. This was
starting to *not* be fun anymore. Was she just
going to change diapers all day?

She picked up Janie with the wet diaper on. Walked over and grabbed a fresh one. Laid Janie back down. Cleaned her. Stuck the diaper under the baby. Folded. Wrapped. Taped. Before anything *else* could happen!

Whew! Tough work!

"How's it going?" Stephanie asked as she strolled in.

"Ta-da!" Michelle showed off her diaper work.

Stephanie hooted with laughter.

"All right—so it's a little droopy," Michelle admitted. "That won't show." She quickly slipped the pink teddy bear pants back on Janie.

Michelle felt proud of her work. And ready for more! "What next?" she asked.

After diapers, anything would be easy!

Chapter 7

♥ *Splat!*

Michelle was in the kitchen, feeding Janie her lunch.

Half of which was now splattered on the ceiling, the counters, the high chair, the floor . . . and Janie.

Yuck! Janie's peas looked like green glop. Janie had squished them with her fork. And wherever the glop landed, it stuck like glue!

"That's quite an arm you've got, Janie," Michelle said. She wet a dish towel and wiped Janie's face. "I see baseball in your future."

"Shell!" Janie shouted, and flung her arms out to the side.

Splat!

Mushed peas smacked Michelle in the face. She licked her lips. "Gross! How can you eat this stuff?"

"Stuff!" Janie shouted.

Splat!

Green peas hit the stove and the window over the sink.

"I get it," Michelle said. "You *don't* eat it. You just fling it all over the kitchen."

Michelle laughed. Maybe she could use that trick next time her dad made something she didn't like!

Janie stuffed some dry Cheerios in her

mouth. One stuck on her cheek. Then she drank some milk from her sippy cup. Milk drooled down from the corners of her mouth.

But Michelle remembered how Nicky and Alex ate when they were babies. So she was used to it. Sort of.

"Look, Janie!" Michelle exclaimed, waving a spoonful of applesauce through the air.

Janie stared in wonder.

"Open wide. Here comes the airplane," Michelle said. "Whee!"

Janie opened her mouth.

Then Michelle "flew" the applesauce into Janie's mouth.

It worked! Janie laughed. And only about half the applesauce dribbled out of her mouth.

"How's it going?" Stephanie asked as she came into the kitchen.

Oops! Michelle wiped up the green glop on the high-chair tray. But there was no way she could hide this mess.

"Not bad," Stephanie commented.

"Really?" Michelle asked.

Stephanie laughed. "Janie usually gets so much food on her, I have to hose her down in the sink! Did she eat anything?"

"A little," Michelle said.

"Then you're doing fine."

Michelle beamed. Stephanie said she was doing fine. Her share of the baby-sitting money was almost in her hands! Would it be enough to finish paying for her T-shirt? If not, maybe she could get another baby-sitting job fast. Especially now that she'd have Stephanie and Mrs. Johnson as references.

"See? I told you, Steph," Michelle said. "I'm good at this. I'm a *born* baby-sitter, right?"

"Right," Stephanie said.

"So, you're going to tell Dad that I can baby-sit alone, right?" Michelle asked.

Stephanie shook her head. "Wrong."

Chapter

8

♥ "What do you mean, wrong?" Michelle exclaimed. "You promised you'd tell Dad I could baby-sit alone."

"No, I didn't," Stephanie insisted. "I told you if you did a good job, I'd tell Dad. That's all. I still think you're too young to baby-sit on your own."

"Too young!" Michelle shrieked. She marched into Janie's room. She was so angry. I'll show her! she thought.

But how? As long as Stephanie is here,

she's still in charge. Even though I'm doing all the work.

What can I do? Michelle wondered. I know I can baby-sit all by myself. I just need a way to prove it.

Michelle glanced at the changing table. At the diaper bag hanging off the side.

Diapers! Michelle thought. Stephanie would have to leave if we were all out of diapers! She'd have to go get more.

Michelle checked the diaper bag, and sighed. It was full. What am I going to do now? she wondered.

Quickly—before she could think about it—Michelle grabbed the bag and pulled out all the diapers. Then she hid them in the bottom drawer of Janie's dresser.

"Stephanie!" Michelle called, hurrying into the living room. "We're out of diapers!"

Stephanie jumped up from the couch. "Are

you sure?" She glanced at her watch. "The Johnsons won't be home for hours!"

Michelle pointed at the diaper bag. "See for yourself."

Stephanie checked the bag. "This is *not* good. These diapers are new and improved. But not *that* improved. One diaper won't last all day."

"Why don't you just run out and get some?" Michelle asked innocently.

"And leave Janie?" Stephanie exclaimed. "I can't!" She frowned. "But we've *got* to have diapers."

Stephanie ran to the telephone. "Maybe somebody at home can get them for us." She dialed the phone.

Oh, no! Michelle hadn't planned on that. She crossed her fingers—on both hands. Please, please let nobody be home!

Stephanie frowned and hung up the phone.

"No luck. I got the answering machine. Where could everyone be?"

Phew! Michelle thought. "I have an idea, Stephanie," she told her sister. "Maybe I could . . . watch Janie by myself. Just for a few minutes."

"No way." Stephanie shook her head.

"But I'm taking great care of Janie now," Michelle declared.

Stephanie didn't look convinced.

"You can run to the supermarket and buy some more diapers," Michelle said. "You'll be back in no time."

Stephanie looked as if she were thinking about it.

"And," Michelle added, "it's almost time for Janie's nap. She'll be asleep almost the whole time you're gone. You'll be back long before Janie even wakes up."

"I don't know, Michelle . . ."

Suddenly Janie started crying.

"What's wrong, sweetheart?" Stephanie asked, reaching out to the baby.

Michelle picked up the little girl. "Janie's wet again," she said. "And there's only one diaper left."

"I thought you said we were all out," Stephanie replied.

"Uh, I did, but I meant, you know, down to the last one," Michelle stuttered. "But after I change her, there won't be any more diapers."

Stephanie sighed. "I guess I have no other choice," she said reluctantly. "I have to go to the store to get more. But, Michelle, you've got to promise to take good care of Janie."

"I will," Michelle said, beaming.

"And keep the doors and windows locked," Stephanie went on. "Don't let anyone in the house."

"I promise," Michelle said.

"And don't forget the emergency numbers," Stephanie reminded her, pointing to the message board by the phone.

Inside, Michelle was thinking, *All right, already!* But aloud she said, "I'll remember. I promise I'll be the best baby-sitter in the whole world."

Stephanie looked worried. But at last she agreed. "I'll run," she said. "I'll be back in a flash." She grabbed her bag and dashed to the front door. Then she turned back to her sister. "Michelle? Don't let me down."

Then she was gone.

"All right!" Michelle cheered. At last—a chance to *prove* she was a great baby-sitter! She was on her own—looking after a baby. All by herself. For the very first time!

Gulp! Michelle suddenly felt nervous.

Then Janie smiled at her. "Shell! Story!"

Hey, Michelle thought. I'll be fine. After all . . .

How hard can it be?

Chapter

9

♥ Michelle changed Janie's diaper. Then she snuggled up with the baby on a quilt on the bedroom floor.

She read the little girl a story, putting in lots of funny voices and sounds. Just like when she read to Nicky and Alex.

This is fun! Michelle thought as Janie cuddled against her.

Soon Janie fell asleep. Michelle carefully slipped out from under her. She slid the book back on Janie's small pink bookshelf.

Should I try to put Janie in her crib? she wondered.

But Janie looked so comfortable where she was. She had her thumb in her mouth and her arm curled around her favorite stuffed bunny. Janie looked as if she could sleep for hours.

Michelle didn't want to wake her up. She laid another blanket over the baby. Then she tiptoed out of the room. She left the door open a few inches so she could hear if Janie woke up.

Piece of cake! Michelle thought. This had to be the best part—taking it easy while the baby sleeps.

She went into the kitchen and got herself a soda, then checked the cabinets. A whole bag of potato chips! All *right!*

Baby-sitting isn't so hard, Michelle decided as she walked into the living room. Anybody could do this.

She flicked on the TV and grabbed a chip from the bag. Then she picked up the phone and dialed Cassie's number.

"Hello?" Cassie answered.

"Hi! It's Michelle. I'm at Mrs. Johnson's house, baby-sitting. I should have the money for my T-shirt in no time!"

"That's awesome," Cassie replied. "Mandy's here. We're going to weed my mom's flower garden. And my mom's going to pay us five dollars each!"

"Cool!" Michelle cried.

"We have to get started," Cassie said. "I'll call you later. Bye!"

Michelle said good-bye and hung up the phone.

Then she turned back to the TV. An old black-and-white mystery was on. Chomping on chips, she was soon lost in the story.

When a commercial came on, Michelle looked around.

She hadn't heard a peep out of Janie. Michelle frowned. How long did babies her age sleep anyway?

She glanced at the clock on the mantel. And where was Stephanie? Shouldn't she be back by now?

Michelle decided she had better check on Janie. She tiptoed into the baby's bedroom.

Janie was still sleeping away on her quilt in the middle of the floor.

She's so cute, Michelle thought. She likes to sleep with the blanket over her head.

Michelle smiled and started to tiptoe out of the room. But then she stopped. A blanket over a baby's head? That's probably not a good idea, Michelle decided. She tiptoed back to the middle of the room.

Only a good baby-sitter would think of

that, Michelle told herself. She reached down and pulled the blanket away from Janie's face.

Michelle gasped.

Janie's stuffed bunny lay in the middle of the quilt.

But Janie was gone!

Chapter

10

♡ Michelle stood frozen for a moment. She stared at the bunny. Then she tossed the blanket aside.

No Janie.

Michelle looked around the room. "Janie?" She must have crawled away. She had to be here somewhere.

Michelle checked under the crib. No Janie.

She checked every corner of the room and beside the chest of drawers. But she didn't find Janie.

Michelle held her breath and threw open the closet doors. She's got to be in—

Crinkle.

Michelle whirled around. The sound came from the living room. The potato chip bag!

Michelle let out a huge sigh of relief. Janie must have crawled out of her room while I was watching the TV, she thought. Now Janie's eating chips!

Michelle ran into the living room. "Janie! Where were you—"

But Janie wasn't there. The potato chip bag crinkled again as it unrolled a little.

Michelle glanced around the room. *Where is Janie?*

"Don't panic!" Michelle whispered to herself. There must be lots of places a little baby could be.

She looked all around the living room. "Janie!" she called. She tried to keep her voice cheerful and friendly. She didn't want to scare Janie.

She checked the kitchen and the Johnsons' bedroom.

Still no Janie.

Now what do I do? Michelle thought.

She ran to the front window and looked out. "Oh, Stephanie—where are you?" she whispered.

Then she ran to the phone and glanced nervously at all the emergency numbers. "I'll call Janie's parents," she whispered, and picked up the phone.

She slammed it down.

Michelle couldn't call the Johnsons. Not yet. They'd freak out—and Stephanie would get in big trouble!

Michelle picked up the phone again. Maybe Dad's home now, she thought.

Slam!

She couldn't call him, either. It would just prove that she doesn't know what she's doing, she thought. That she's too little to baby-sit. And she'd *still* get Stephanie in trouble.

Besides, Janie had to be here *somewhere*, she told herself. Babies don't just disappear, right?

Michelle ran back to the window to see if Stephanie was coming down the sidewalk. But all she saw was an old lady walking her poodle.

What could be taking her sister so long? "Hurry, Stephanie!" she cried.

Wait a minute, she thought. If Stephanie comes back before I find Janie—*I'll* be in big trouble!

What should she do?

Michelle dashed to the kitchen. Where were those emergency phone numbers? She spotted them on the bulletin board by the phone.

What about 911? she wondered. Should she call? She knew that was only for emergencies. But this sure felt like an emergency to her!

She laid a shaky hand on the receiver, trying to decide what to do.

Riiiiiing!

Michelle jumped back. Who could that be?

What if it's Janie's mom? she thought. Mrs. Johnson said she might call to make sure everything was okay.

Oh, no! What am I going to tell her?

Riiiiiing!

She stared at the telephone.

Then she took a deep breath and picked up the receiver.

"H-hello?" she said in a trembling voice.

Chapter
11

♥ "Hello? Michelle? Is that you?" a familiar voice asked.

Michelle sank into a chair, clutching the telephone to her ear. "Cassie?" she asked.

"And me, too," Mandy added.

"We called back to ask you—when do you want to go get the T-shirts?" Cassie said.

"I . . ."

"Michelle," Mandy asked. "Are you all right?"

"Yes, I—" Michelle's voice broke. "No, I'm not. I'm *terrible!*"

"What's wrong?" Cassie asked.

"You won't believe this," Michelle cried. "But—I lost the baby!"

"What!" both girls exclaimed.

Michelle told her friends everything. "And I don't know what to do. Should I call 911?"

"I don't think so," Mandy said. "I mean, she's got to be there—somewhere."

"We'll come over right away," Cassie said. "We'll help you look for her."

"Okay," Michelle said. "But hurry!"

Michelle stood by the window, waiting. Cassie and Mandy arrived a few minutes later.

"Where did you last see her?" Mandy asked the moment Michelle opened the front door.

Michelle led them to Janie's room. The

girls decided to start their search from there.

"Janie! Janie, where are you?" Mandy started calling.

"I know," Michelle said. "Let's try calling out *ice cream.*"

"Ice cream?" Cassie asked.

"It's Janie's favorite food," Michelle explained. But that didn't work.

Next Michelle tried playing Janie's favorite video. "Maybe she'll hear it and come to watch."

Music for preschoolers filled the air. But Janie didn't come running.

"Do you think Janie could have opened a door and gotten out of the house?" Mandy asked.

"I don't know," Michelle said with a worried frown. "Can little kids her age do that?"

Nicky and Alex were four years old now. Michelle couldn't remember exactly what they could and couldn't do back when they were only two.

I wish I'd read that book Stephanie gave me, Michelle thought miserably. I wish I'd asked her more questions about Janie.

"We'd better check outside," Michelle said. "Just in case."

She and her friends hurried through the family room and out the door to the back-yard. Michelle found a swing set with a swing gently swaying in the breeze.

Was it the wind? Or had Janie just been swinging in it?

The sandbox had little baby footprints in it. Could Janie have come this way? Or were the footprints old?

"Michelle," Cassie said. "Do you think . . ."

"What?"

Cassie bit her lip. "Do you think Janie could have gotten out of the yard?"

Oh, no! Michelle ran to the back fence to check the gate. It was locked securely. She gazed across the backyard. There didn't seem to be anyplace where a baby could sneak out.

"I don't think she came out here," Michelle said at last.

"So now what do we do?" Mandy asked.

"Janie must still be in the house," Michelle replied. "Somewhere."

"But didn't we look everywhere?" Cassie asked.

"Let's check everything twice, okay?" Michelle's lip began to tremble.

Now she understood what baby-sitting was really all about.

It's not about making extra money so to buy stuff, she thought. It's not about reading fairy tales. Or playing games and having fun. It's not even about changing icky diapers.

It's about making sure that somebody's child is happy and safe while the parents are away.

How hard could it be?

Really, *really* hard. Michelle thought miserably.

"Come on, guys," Michelle said as she led her friends back into the house. "We've got to keep looking."

Once inside, they heard the front door slam.

"Janie!" Michelle exclaimed. Could a little kid her age open the front door by herself?

Michelle ran through the house and into the living room.

But it wasn't Janie.

It was Stephanie. She was back from the store. She stood in the middle of the living room with a package of diapers under her arm.

"Hi, Michelle. I'm back. Sorry it took so long. You wouldn't believe the lines. They were awful!" She dropped her bag on the couch and looked around. "How's Janie? Is everything okay?"

Chapter

12

♡ Michelle stared at Stephanie. She didn't know what to say.

"How's Janie?" Stephanie asked again. Then she frowned. "Michelle—why are you looking at me like that?"

"Well, I . . . uh . . ." Maybe she could talk to Stephanie while Cassie and Mandy kept looking. Maybe . . .

It was no use. Michelle was scared. She needed Stephanie's help!

Michelle burst into tears.

"What's wrong?" Stephanie put an arm around Michelle.

"I lost the baby!" Michelle blurted out. She shook her head as tears spilled down her cheeks. Janie's gone, and it's all my fault, she thought. Now Stephanie is going to kill me!

Stephanie put her hands on Michelle's shoulders. "Tell me exactly what happened," she said gently.

Michelle couldn't believe it. Stephanie didn't look freaked out, the way Michelle felt.

She looks the way Dad does, Michelle thought. When he's taking care of something that went wrong. Calm. Serious. Taking control.

Michelle told Stephanie everything. How Janie fell asleep in the middle of the floor. How Michelle left her there to take her nap.

How she had a snack and watched TV. And how she and Cassie and Mandy looked everywhere for her even outside.

Michelle even told Stephanie how she tricked her into going to the store for diapers. Just so Michelle could prove she could baby-sit all by herself.

Then she waited for Stephanie to yell at her.

But instead Stephanie ran into Janie's room.

"She's not in there," Michelle told her. "I checked a million times already."

Stephanie opened the closet doors.

"But I looked there already," Michelle protested. She gazed past Stephanie at the mound of stuffed animals piled in a corner of the closet.

Stephanie stooped down and moved aside a few of them.

There, hiding among her toys was Janie, fast asleep.

"Janie!" Michelle breathed. She kneeled down and gently brushed some blond curls off the baby's forehead. "You're okay."

"Oh, Steph," Michelle whispered. "I was so scared." She stepped out of the closet. "How did you know? How did you know she'd be here?"

"Her parents told me," Stephanie said. "They said sometimes she likes to crawl in there and nap with her stuffed animals."

Janie's eyes slowly fluttered open.

"Shell?" she said sleepily.

"Hi, pumpkin." Michelle reached for the little girl and hugged her tight.

Janie had been safe and sound all along!

Then Michelle remembered her friends. Cassie and Mandy were waiting nervously in the living room.

"Look who I found," Michelle said, leading Janie into the room.

"Janie!" Cassie exclaimed.

"Hi, sweetie," Mandy said, smiling at the baby.

Janie smiled back and poked her thumb in her mouth. Then she hid shyly behind Michelle.

"How come Stephanie isn't mad at you?" Cassie whispered in Michelle's ear.

"Because," Michelle replied, "Janie was here all along. She was just napping in her closet."

"Well, we'd better go," Mandy told Michelle. "Call us later, okay?"

Michelle nodded and closed the door behind her friends. Then she flopped down on the living room couch and sighed.

Stephanie came in the room with Janie's bucket of blocks. She helped Janie build a castle on the floor.

"So—are you okay?" she asked Michelle. "I guess Janie gave you a little scare."

Michelle groaned. "Baby-sitting is a *lot* harder than it looks!"

Stephanie nodded. "That's the truth."

Michelle sat down on the floor and added a tiny tower to the side of Janie's castle.

"Listen, Michelle," Stephanie went on. "I'm really not trying to be mean to you about baby-sitting. And I'm not trying to keep all the jobs to myself. Baby-sitting is a really cool job. But it's not easy. It's a big responsibility. I don't think I would have been ready to do it when I was your age."

"I don't think I am, either," Michelle said. "And after today, I don't know if I'll *ever* be ready!"

That night at dinner Danny dumped a huge serving of peas onto Michelle's plate.

Michelle stared at the little green balls and wrinkled her nose. She used to like peas. But after seeing Janie eating them today, Michelle wasn't sure if she could ever eat peas again!

"So," Danny said, smiling brightly at Stephanie and Michelle. "How did the baby-sitting go?"

Michelle gulped. She stared at her sister. Stephanie wouldn't say anything about Michelle losing the baby. Would she?

Stephanie put down her spoon and leaned forward. "Let me tell you what Michelle did. . . ."

Oh, no! What was Stephanie doing? Michelle wondered. Stephanie had been so nice and understanding this afternoon.

Now, after all that . . .

Was Stephanie going to rat on her?

Chapter

13

♥ Michelle closed her eyes and waited for Stephanie to tell on her. To say that she was a horrible baby-sitter.

"Michelle did a great job with Janie today," Stephanie announced.

Michelle opened one eye. "I did *what?*"

Stephanie smiled at Michelle. "I let her do everything, so she could see what it was really like. She changed Janie's diapers—"

Uncle Jesse's fork clattered to his plate. "You're kidding!" he teased.

Stephanie laughed. "Nope. In fact, she changed Janie three times."

"Then she's a lot braver than I am," Uncle Joey joked.

"But she did a lot more than that," Stephanie went on. "She fed Janie lunch. She read her stories and played with her. She did great. She really earned her half of the baby-sitting money."

"Michelle," her father said. "I'm really proud of you."

"I guess all that training with the twins really paid off," Aunt Becky said.

"I guess . . ." Michelle said slowly. So when was Stephanie going to tell about how she lost the baby?

Stephanie took a long drink of milk. "One more thing . . ." she said, wiping her mouth with a napkin.

Uh-oh, here it comes, Michelle thought.

"Janie is crazy about Michelle," Stephanie said. "And that's the best reference a baby-sitter can have." She gave Michelle a pat on the back. "I think that one day—when she's a little older—Michelle is going to make an awesome baby-sitter!"

Michelle squeezed her sister's hand under the table. "Thanks, Steph."

Later that evening Michelle found Stephanie reading a book in the room they shared.

Michelle sat down at the foot of her sister's bed. "So, Stephanie," Michelle asked her. "How come you didn't tell?"

"Tell them what?" Stephanie asked.

"You know," Michelle said. She lowered her voice to a whisper. "That I *lost* the *baby!*"

Stephanie slipped a bookmark into her book and sat up. "But you *didn't* lose the baby, Michelle. Janie was fine the whole time."

"But I *thought* she was lost," Michelle said. "And I didn't know what to do."

"I know," Stephanie said. "But I have to accept a lot of the blame, too. I really shouldn't have left the baby—no matter what. And I shouldn't have left you alone with her. Not even for diapers. You were really great with Janie. But, well, you're just not ready to baby-sit. We're lucky nothing happened. And I hope you learned your lesson, too."

"I did," Michelle said. "Three of them."

"Three?" Stephanie asked.

Michelle counted on her fingers. "It's not good to trick your big sister. And when things go wrong, you should call somebody. That's what the emergency phone numbers are for."

"You said three," Stephanie pointed out. "What's the third thing you learned?"

Michelle grinned. "That it's a lot easier earning money by washing cars and doing laundry!"

A week later, on Sunday afternoon, Michelle and her family went to the park to skate. Cassie and Mandy came along, too.

And they all wore their brand-new matching T-shirts!

Cassie and Mandy bought their shirts with the money they earned doing chores. And Michelle used the twenty dollars she made from baby-sitting with Stephanie to get hers.

"I'm *never* going to take this shirt off!" Michelle declared as she skated around her friends.

"Even when you sleep?" Cassie asked with a giggle.

"*Even* when I sleep."

"Not even when it gets dirty?" Mandy teased.

"Well, maybe I'll take it off to wash it," Michelle admitted. "Or maybe I could wash it by wearing it into the shower!"

Her friends laughed.

Then Michelle spotted Stephanie talking to a woman pushing a baby stroller. Why is Stephanie pointing at me? she wondered.

Stephanie skated over and grabbed Michelle by the hand. "Come on," she said. "I want you to meet Mrs. Anders. She needs a baby-sitter next Saturday afternoon, and—"

"But, Steph!" Michelle protested. "I can't baby-sit!"

"Yes, you can," Stephanie said with a grin.

"But I thought . . ."

"Mrs. Anders has three boys," Stephanie explained. "I'm outnumbered. I could really use some help. And you *are* my assistant baby-sitter, right?"

Michelle looked at her sister and smiled. "I guess I am."

FULL HOUSE™
SISTERS

A brand-new series starring Stephanie AND Michelle!

#1 Two On The Town

Stephanie and Michelle find themselves
in the big city—and in big trouble!

#2 One Boss Too Many

Stephanie and Michelle think camp will be major fun.
If only these two sisters were getting along!

When sisters get together...expect the unexpected!

A MINSTREL®BOOK

Published by Pocket Books   2012-01

FULL HOUSE Stephanie™

PHONE CALL FROM A FLAMINGO	
THE BOY-OH-BOY NEXT DOOR	88004-7/$3.99
TWIN TROUBLES	88121-3/$3.99
HIP HOP TILL YOU DROP	88290-2/$3.99
HERE COMES THE BRAND NEW ME	88291-0/$3.99
THE SECRET'S OUT	89858-2/$3.99
DADDY'S NOT-SO-LITTLE GIRL	89859-0/$3.99
P.S. FRIENDS FOREVER	89860-4/$3.99
GETTING EVEN WITH THE FLAMINGOES	89861-2/$3.99
THE DUDE OF MY DREAMS	52273-6/$3.99
BACK-TO-SCHOOL COOL	52274-4/$3.99
PICTURE ME FAMOUS	52275-2/$3.99
TWO-FOR-ONE CHRISTMAS FUN	52276-0/$3.99
THE BIG FIX-UP MIX-UP	53546-3/$3.99
TEN WAYS TO WRECK A DATE	53547-1/$3.99
WISH UPON A VCR	53548-X/$3.99
DOUBLES OR NOTHING	53549-8/$3.99
SUGAR AND SPICE ADVICE	56841-8/$3.99
NEVER TRUST A FLAMINGO	56842-6/$3.99
THE TRUTH ABOUT BOYS	56843-4/$3.99
CRAZY ABOUT THE FUTURE	00361-5/$3.99
MY SECRET ADMIRER	00362-3/$3.99
BLUE RIBBON CHRISTMAS	00363-1/$3.99
THE STORY ON OLDER BOYS	00830-7/$3.99
MY THREE WEEKS AS A SPY	00831-5/$3.99
NO BUSINESS LIKE SHOW BUSINESS	00832-3/$3.99
MAIL-ORDER BROTHER	01725-X/$3.99
TO CHEAT OR NOT TO CHEAT	01726-8/$3.99
WINNING IS EVERYTHING	01727-6/$3.99
HELLO BIRTHDAY, GOOD-BYE FRIEND	02098-6/$3.99
	02160-5/$3.99

Available from Minstrel® Books Published by Pocket Books

Simon & Schuster Mail Order Dept. BWB
200 Old Tappan Rd., Old Tappan, N.J. 07675

Please send me the books I have checked above. I am enclosing $_____ (please add $0.75 to cover the postage and handling for each order. Please add appropriate sales tax). Send check or money order--no cash or C.O.D.'s please. Allow up to six weeks for delivery. For purchase over $10.00 you may use VISA: card number, expiration date and customer signature must be included.

Name _____

Address _____

City _____ State/Zip _____

VISA Card # _____ Exp.Date _____

Signature _____

929-26